P9-DHS-058

BATMAN™

THE PENGUIN'S ARCTIC ADVENTURE

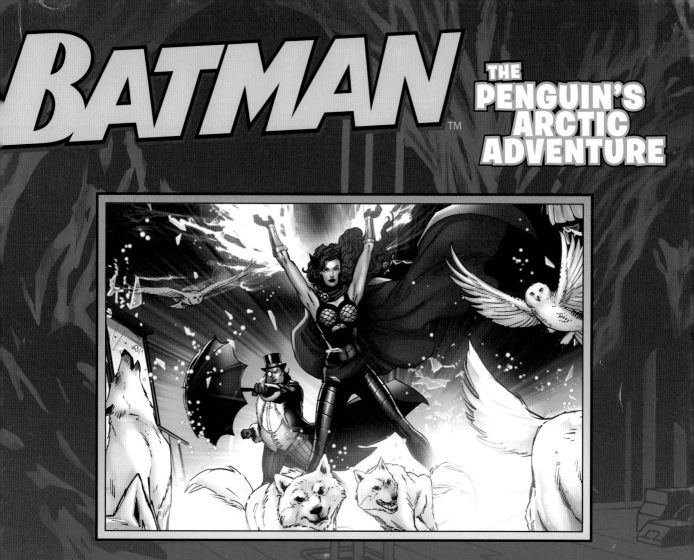

BY **DONALD LEMKE**

ILLUSTRATED BY **JEREMY ROBERTS**

Batman created by Bob Kane

HARPER FESTIVAL

An Imprint of HarperCollinsPublishers

THE HEROES AND VILLAINS IN THIS BOOK!

THE PENGUIN

Oswald Cobblepot, known as the Penguin, is a wealthy businessman in Gotham City. He is also a fowl criminal who carries a trick umbrella as a weapon.

CIRCE

Circe is a sorceress from Greek mythology. With powerful spells, this goddess often changes humans to animals.

HarperFestival is an imprint of HarperCollins Publishers.
Batman: The Penguin's Arctic Adventure
Copyright © 2015 DC Comics.
BATMAN and all related characters and elements are trademarks of and © DC Comics.
(s15)
HARP30904

Manufactured in China.
No part of this book may be used or reproduced in any manner whatsoever without written permission except in the case of brief quotations embodied in critical articles and reviews.
For information address HarperCollins Children's Books, a division of HarperCollins Publishers, 195 Broadway, New York, NY 10007.
www.harpercollinschildrens.com

Library of Congress catalog card number: 2014935754
ISBN 978-0-06-221000-5

14 15 16 17 18 SCP 10 9 8 7 6 5 4 3 2 1
❖
First Edition

BATMAN

Orphaned as a child, young Bruce Wayne trained his body and mind to become Batman, the Dark Knight. He is an expert martial artist, crime fighter, and detective. Using high-tech gadgets and weapons, Batman fights against the most dangerous criminals in Gotham City.

ROBIN

Damian Wayne was already a fierce warrior when he first met his father—Batman. With the help of the Dark Knight, Damian honed his skills and now he uses his mastery of martial arts to fight crime at his father's side as Robin.

ZATANNA

Zatanna is a powerful magician and super hero. This Master of Magic casts her spells by speaking words backward.

On a warm spring evening, a crowd gathers in downtown Gotham City. Businessman Oswald Cobblepot, known as the Penguin, is opening an animal exhibit called Arctic Adventure.

A ribbon hangs across the entrance. The Penguin holds up a pair of oversized scissors. "Thanks to all who donated to these exhibits," he says. "Now enjoy an adventure into the arctic!" He cuts the ribbon, and the crowd funnels inside.

Billionaire Bruce Wayne is among them. He walks past arctic wolves and polar bears, and finally stops at an exhibit of a rare snowy owl.

"A donation from Tim Wiseman," explains the Penguin. He hands Bruce a list of the zoo's gift givers, and then turns toward the owl. "Creatures of the night, aren't they?"

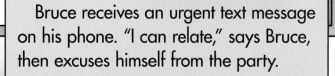

Bruce receives an urgent text message on his phone. "I can relate," says Bruce, then excuses himself from the party.

Bruce returns to Wayne Manor. Deep below the mansion is the headquarters of his secret identity, Batman. His crime-fighting partner Robin stands near the Batcomputer.

"Another business owner has disappeared," says Robin. The Boy Wonder displays a missing persons list on the high-tech computer screen.
The World's Greatest Detective recognizes the name Tim Wiseman.

"Do you know him?" asks Robin, curious.
"No," replies Batman, "but something tells me he's a real night owl."

After the party ends, Batman and Robin sneak into Arctic Adventure. The names on each exhibit match the names on the missing persons list. At the end of a long hallway is an empty cage. Its sign reads: Donated by Bruce Wayne.

Hoo! Hoo! Behind them, the snowy owl lets out a hoot.

The Dynamic Duo spins, and they spot the Penguin.
Beside him stands the evil sorceress Circe!
Batman quickly presses a button on his high-tech
Utility Belt, signaling for backup.

"I'm afraid that exhibit is reserved," Circe tells the Dynamic Duo. "But this zoo could always use another bat and a bird!" The sorceress blasts a powerful spell from her hand.

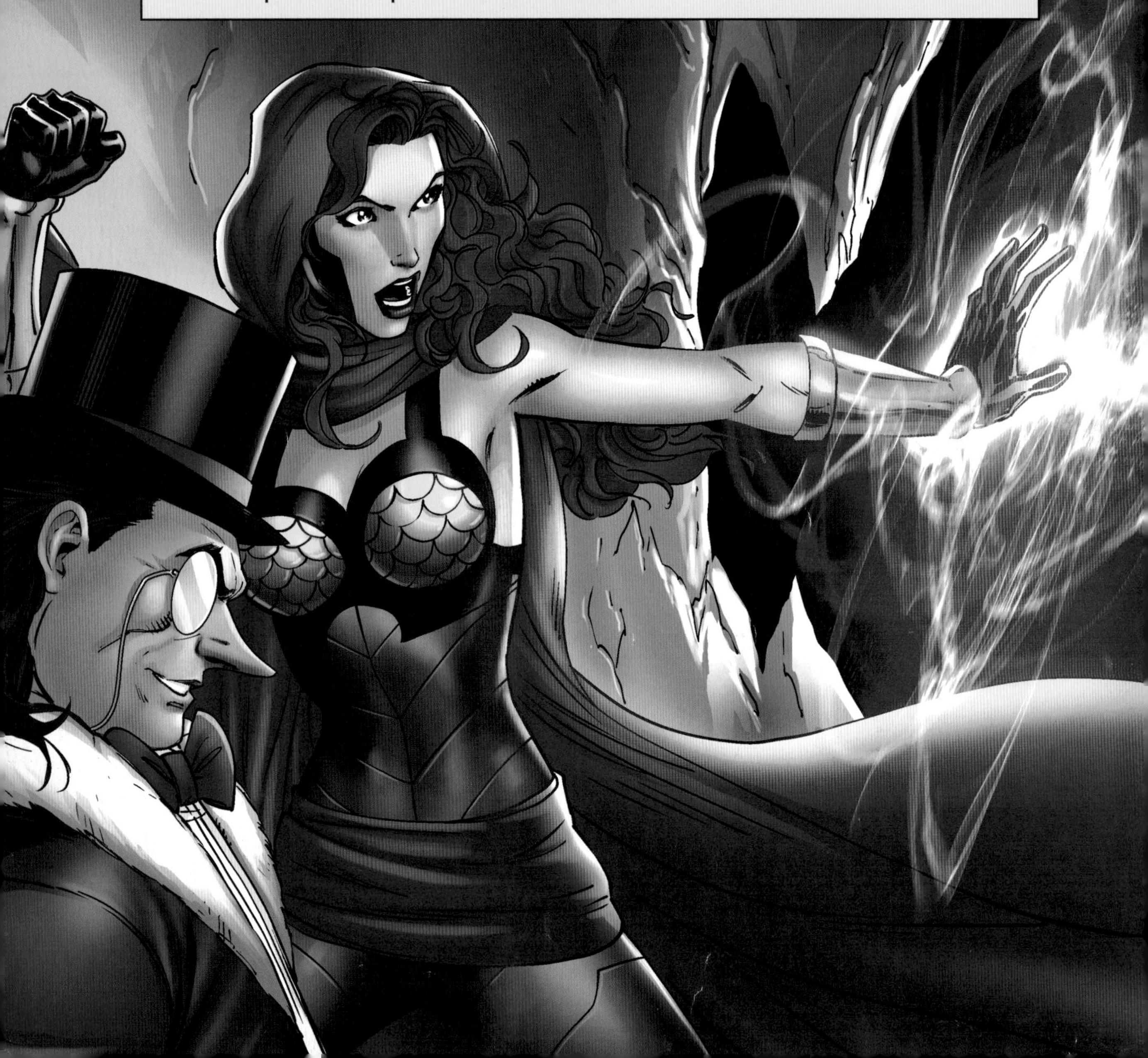

The spell strikes the super heroes. The Dynamic Duo transform into a real bat and robin.

"HA-HA-HA!" Circe lets out an evil laugh. "With this army of animals," she says, "I'll reign over Gotham City's underworld!"

"And with my competition out of the way," adds the Penguin, "I'll rule the city's business world!"

Suddenly, a purple puff of smoke explodes in the room. When it clears, Zatanna stands in its place. "Not so fast!" says the Master of Magic.

Zatanna twirls her hands above her head. Then she points at the two high-flying heroes and shouts a spell. *"Oud cimanyd!"*

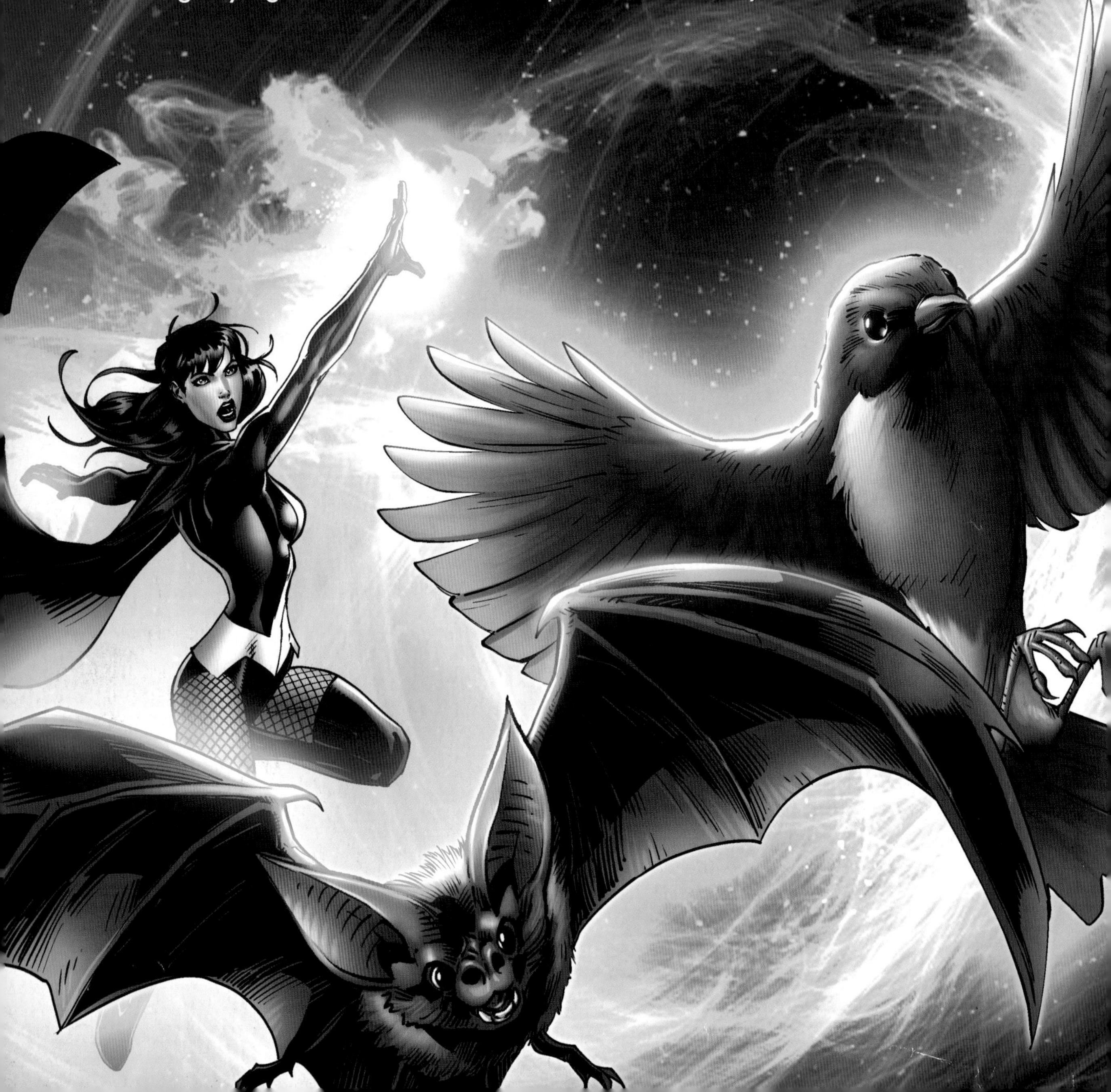

Batman and Robin instantly change back into their normal, heroic forms.

"Now what's the plan?" asks Zatanna.

The Boy Wonder shrugs. "I kind of thought we'd just wing it," he jokes.

Circe raises her arms toward the heavens. From head to toe, her body glows with magical energy. "Arctic attack!" she shouts. The animal exhibits suddenly spring open. Wolves, foxes, polar bears, and owls rush from their cages.

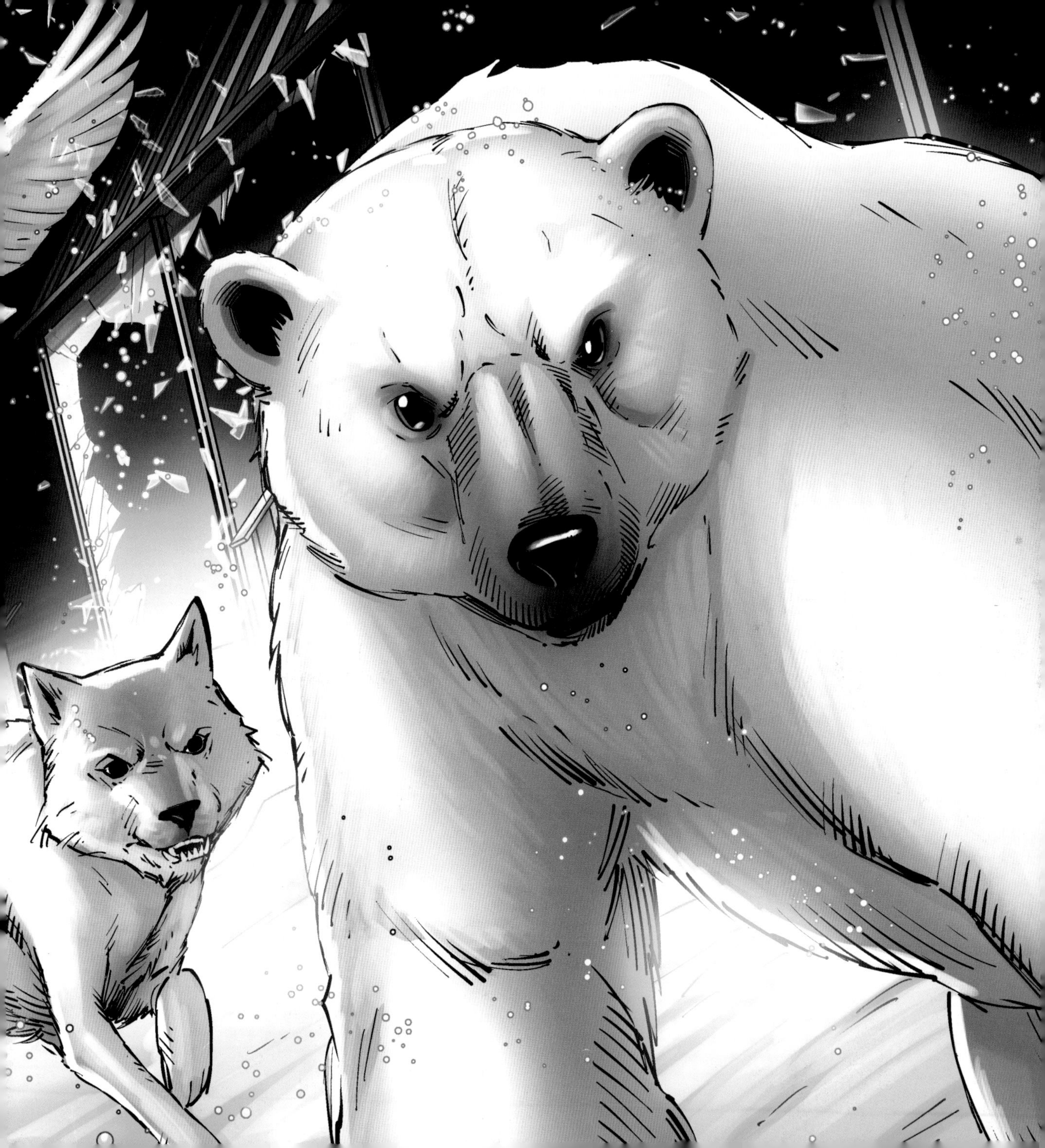

Zatanna steps forward. The Master of Magic attempts another spell. *"Namuh nrut!"* This time, her magic doesn't work.

Circe laughs again. "Your street magic is no match for a goddess," she says, doubling the strength of her sorcery.

Batman removes the grapnel gun from his Utility Belt.
He fires the gun's metal hook into the ceiling.

"Then she'll need a little boost!" says Batman. He
grabs Zatanna, and the Batrope pulls them into the air.
With the skills of an acrobat, Robin spins, jumps, and
flips to avoid the arctic animals racing toward him.

From high above, Zatanna unleashes another spell. She traps Circe and the Penguin inside a magical cage with the dangerous animals.

The Penguin pulls out his trick umbrella. He fires the weapon at the cage, again and again. *Bang! Bang!* The noise angers the animals. They turn on the two evildoers.

"Stop, you fool!" yells Circe. As the animals approach, the sorceress has no choice but to reverse her own spell.

Moments later, Zatanna releases the missing business owners from the cage. They thank the World's Greatest Heroes for saving them.

"How did you know that plan would work?" Robin asks his crime-fighting partner.

The Dark Knight smiles. "Animal instincts, I guess," Batman replies.